To Elena Contreras,
with gratitude for her endless
wisdom and generosity

Special thanks to Mary Lee Donovan, Melanie Córdova, and Maryellen Hanley at Candlewick Press. I'm extremely grateful for your guidance and encouragement. What a fun, enriching, and smooth ride!

• • •

_____ First edition 2023

Library of Congress Catalog Card Number 2022908655
ISBN 978-1-5362-1635-6 (English hardcover)
ISBN 978-1-5362-1641-7 (Spanish hardcover)
ISBN 978-1-5362-3250-9 (English-Spanish hardcover)

22 23 24 25 26 27 CCP 10 9 8 7 6 5 4 3 2 1

Printed in Shenzhen, Guangdong, China

This book was typeset in Avenir.
The illustrations were created digitally.

Candlewick Press
99 Dover Street
Somerville, Massachusetts 02144

www.candlewick.com

ELENA
Rides

JUANA MEDINA

CANDLEWICK PRESS

Elena wants to ride.
Elena buckles her helmet.

She readies,
she steadies . . .

she pushes,
she pedals!

She wobbles
and bobbles...

Elena tries again.

She tries and tries . . .

Elena cries!

She bawls!

Elena sighs . . .
and sits awhile.

Elena dries her eyes . . .

and tries, tries, tries!

Elena slides!

Elena glides!

She flies, she goes.

She goes, goes, **goes!**

Fast! Fast!
Even faster!

Elena does not ride.
Elena says N-O: **NO!**

Elena dusts off.

She goes up and down

and all around.

Elena rides!